This book belongs to:

....

A NEW BURLINGTON BOOK
The Old Brewery
6 Blundell Street
London N7 9BH

Consultant: Barbara Taylor
Editor: Lauren Taylor
Designer: Elaine Wilkinson

First published in the UK in 2012 by
QED Publishing
A Quarto Group company
230 City Road
London EC1V 2TT

www.qed-publishing.co.uk

A catalogue record for this book is available from the British Library.

ISBN 978 1 78171 013 5

Printed in China

Rabbit's Spring Adventure

Anita Loughrey

and Daniel Howarth

NEW
BURLINGTON
BOOKS

Rabbit poked his nose out of his warren.
Bright yellow and purple flowers
swayed in the breeze.

Rabbit's big sister had told
him it was finally spring.

But what did that mean?
He had to find out!

Rabbit hopped into the wood. Blossom covered the trees and grass. Tiny green buds were on the branches of the trees.

There was
so much
to discover!

Rabbit hopped so far that he was soon tired out.
He stopped and looked around.
Where was he?

"Oh no!"
cried Rabbit.
"I'm lost."

Suddenly, Rabbit jumped up
and thumped his back foot.
He could hear splashing.

"What's that sound?" he asked,
and hopped to the pond.

On the pond, Frog was jumping on the lily pads.

Rabbit peered into the water.
He saw some frogspawn bobbing on the surface.
"What's wrong, Rabbit?" asked Frog.

"I'm lost," said Rabbit.
"Do you know
where my home is?"
But Frog didn't.

Rabbit hopped to the cornfield,
where seeds were sprouting into new plants.
Rabbit heard a rustle.

"What's that sound?"
he asked.

Mouse scampered out of the corn.
She had woken up from her long winter sleep
and was searching for food.

"Do you know where my home is?"
asked Rabbit. But Mouse didn't.

Rabbit hopped back
into the wood.
He could hear chirping
in the trees.

"What's that sound?"
he asked.

He looked up and saw Owl watching
over her nest. Her little owlets had hatched.

"Do you know where my home is?" asked Rabbit.
"It can't be far away," said Owl.

"Everything looks so different," said Rabbit.
"And there are so many new sounds.
I don't think I'll ever get home."

"Close your eyes and listen carefully," said Owl.
"I'm sure you'll hear something familiar."

So Rabbit did...
He could hear laughter nearby!
"What's that sound?" he asked.

Rabbit hopped through
the trees and soon saw his
brothers and sisters playing
outside in the sunshine.

Rabbit's big sister hopped over to him.
"Did you find out what happens in spring?"
she asked.

"Spring is very beautiful," said Rabbit.
"But it will take some getting used to!"

Spring activities

Fun and simple ideas for you and your child to explore together.

Decorate eggs with bright spring colours.
Boil the eggs with a little white vinegar for
10 minutes, then let the eggs cool.
Refrigerate the eggs for at least
one hour and then paint
with watercolours.

Press some spring flowers. Make sure
the flowers you choose are fresh and
completely dry. Place the flowers
between two sheets of paper, slot
them between the middle pages of
a large book, close the book, and
then rest a heavy object on top.
In about 2 weeks' time your
flowers should be ready.

Grow some spring plants in a window box. All you need is some soil, some bulbs or seeds and plenty of sunshine and water. Ask at your local garden centre for the best type of plants to choose. You could choose your child's favourite colour for the flowers, or plants with interesting scents.

Act out the story with your child. Use paper, pens, pencils and paints to make masks of Rabbit and his friends. Can your child remember anything the characters said? Does your child want to act out the story as it is in the book, or do they want to change the story in their own way?

What did we learn about spring?

Rabbit sees the first flowers pushing their way through the soil. In spring, plants often grow from bulbs. The food stored in bulbs provides the energy to sprout leaves and flowers quickly, before other plants start growing.

Rabbit notices the buds on tree branches. These buds burst open and bright green leaves unfold and stretch out to soak up the sun. The leaves trap the sun's energy and use this energy to make food for the tree.

Frogspawn is bobbing on the pond. Frogspawn is made of lots of frogs' eggs inside balls of jelly, which are all stuck together. The frogspawn floats on the surface of the pond, where the warm water and sunshine help the eggs to develop. Tadpoles grow inside the eggs then wriggle out after about ten days. The tadpoles then grow legs, lose their tails and turn into baby frogs.

Spring is a warm, bright season. It is also rainy. It is a time when farmers plant seeds in their fields. The warm sunshine and spring rain help the seeds to sprout. Roots grow down into the soil and leaves grow up towards the sunlight.

Owl's owlets hatch out of their eggs. Baby birds hatch in spring. They will have plenty of time to grow big and strong before the cold winter season arrives. They have fluffy down feathers at first and grow their proper flying feathers later on.